**Please return / renew
this item by the last date shown**

**Items may be renewed
by telephone**

East
Renfrewshire
COUNCIL

First published in Great Britain by Barrington Stoke Ltd
10 Belford Terrace, Edinburgh EH4 3DQ
Copyright © 2002 Lesley Howarth

ISBN 1-84299-043-8
Printed by Polestar AUP Aberdeen Ltd

A Note from the Author

I grew up in the holiday town of Bournemouth, so I remember the crowds in summer, and the way the town 'shut down' in winter – the empty beaches, closed clubs, the feeling of nowhere to go.

Cornwall suffers from the same 'winter blues'. It's a beautiful place for a holiday, but there's not much for young people to do in winter. I felt sure that young people would recognise Jem's boredom when looking for a job – so I started the story of a boy in a tourist town that 'dies' in winter. It would be a surfing story, and it would take Jem to new places in his life, both literally, and in his imagination.

I had picked daffodils myself as a casual job, so I knew what it would be like for Jem. I hoped his life would open out when he rode a wave on Dade County's surfboard, so that if he ever picked daffodils again, he would know that he had a choice.

Contents

Chapter 1
Surfies

We'd walked up the hill from Hellbay. My friend Stoney and I were crossing the cliff-top car park, when a man burst out of a camper van. He looked us up and down. We weren't doing anything. We were just walking behind his van.

"Did you two lads snap my aerial off?" he scowled.

"No," Stoney said.

"It's funny how things go missing," he said, "and turn up later, in town."

"Nothing to do with us," I said.

I thought he was going to punch me. He wasn't friendly at all, like the usual visiting surfers who lived in the Hellbay car park for half the year. Yet his van was topped with surfboards.

"I'll let you go, then," he said. "But stay away from my van."

We could feel his eyes on us as we turned onto the cliff path on the other side of the car park.

"I thought he was going to hit us," I said.

"If that's a good day," Stoney said, "I'd hate to meet him on a bad day."

We avoided the car park after that. As far as we knew, the angry bloke lived there. Sometimes we saw him jogging along the beach. He wasn't like other surfers. He wasn't one of the local 'crew'. He wasn't one of the international surfers we see every summer either – at least, not one that we recognised.

"It's a bit late for surfers," I said.

"Or early for next year," Stoney said, "with three months of winter ahead of us."

Some local surfers still go out on good days in winter. But the tanned professional surfers, who surf all over the world, turn up in the Hellbay car park at about the same time, every year. They live out of their camper vans all summer and eat at the pub where I work. *The Lobster Pot* gets all the 'surfies'. We serve the best fresh fish, plus we show live surfing competitions on satellite TV.

You can always tell a surfer's car because it's covered in wetsuits hanging out to dry, and topped with surfboards. The best surfers

look at the waves. Then they take out a
board and paddle out to the 'beachbreak'.
A beachbreak is the point where the waves
break on the beach. In summer the surfers
line up closely. They look like flies from the
cliff-top.

For a long time after the angry bloke
burst out of his van, Stoney and I walked
round the car park to reach the next bay.

Devil's Point, they call it.

At Devil's Point there's a café with a fruit
machine. Stoney and I had watched lots of
people play it. We knew when to hold the
raspberries, and when to spin them. We knew
which combinations of fruit made the
machine cough up money. The owner of the
café didn't like us going over there too often.
My mother didn't like it, either.

"Where are you going?" she'd say.

"Fishing, or something, I don't know."
I didn't know, myself.

4

"You're going over to Devil's Point to play that fruit machine again, aren't you?"

"What else would you like me to do in winter?" I'd say.

"Work a bit harder at getting a job?" she'd snap back.

"What for?" I'd say. "It's not like there's any point."

All the good jobs are 'upcountry', as they say. What they mean is, miles from here. Cornwall looks pretty in summer. But try living here all year.

This place is a dead end in winter. In summer, it's holiday heaven – gorgeous beaches, picture-postcard cottages, the kind of place everyone dreams of. That's because they don't have to live here. They never see the darker side. I've had a few mates with drug problems. There isn't much else to do. Sometimes it feels like I'll never escape.

Like I'll spend the rest of my life here, watching telly.

You wouldn't think anyone would want to escape from Hellbay. People come from all over the world to surf at our beaches. We're on the international surfing map, here. But I was born and bred here, and none of my mates surf.

Surfies were always in a separate gang, at school. They wore their hair in dreadlocks and got into trouble over it, in class. They bought gear with expensive labels like 'Wipeout' and 'Zing!' in surf shops and spent their time on the beach.

Some of the local surfing crew were in the year above me. Most of them were losers who stayed on here instead of leaving Hellbay as soon as they left school. I'm going to escape, one day. Stoney will, too. No matter how long it takes us.

Stoney and me were in the 'townies' gang in school. We never mixed with the surfies. We went to different cafés. Townies were into fishing. Surfies spent all their time talking about 'gnarly swells'.

"What *is* a gnarly swell?" I asked Stoney the other day, as we were fishing off Devil's Point.

"I think it means big waves," Stoney said. "Where did you hear it?"

"Gull told me," I said. "That surfer who comes into the pub. He tells me what they say."

"Gull's all right," Stoney said. "Maybe he means the rip current. It looks pretty gnarly to me."

A 'rip current' is a strong current of water that will sweep you out to sea. There's a strong rip current, right across the bay.

From the top of the cliffs it looks like a ruffled stretch of water. You can't fight that rip current. It'll take you out to sea and keep you there until it drowns you. It always amazes me that the surfers aren't afraid to cross it. They'll paddle right over that rip as though it doesn't exist, surf all summer, then walk away.

But they don't have to live with that rip. Or with the town of Hellbay.

Chapter 2
Hellbay

Me and Stoney, we're stuck here. The only thing to do is to go fishing, but there's hardly any fish.

When you're sixteen and you can leave school, anyone who wants a career leaves Hellbay. Or you can stay and get a summer job, and sign on for the winter. That's what most people do. The longer you stay, the more stuck you get. One day, I'll look like my dad.

Surfies don't care what they do. They hang around on the beach and take any jobs that turn up. The international surfers who come here every year can afford to surf all summer. Their surfboards and wetsuits are top-of-the-range. Some surfers return every year, with stories about top surfing spots around the world, and competitions they've taken part in. I work at the pub, I hear all the stories. You should hear them talk.

There are two pubs in Hellbay, *The Lobster Pot* and *The Oyster Catcher*. I work at *The Lobster Pot* sometimes. That's how I hear the stories. I know that the best surfing beach in Hawaii is called 'Jaws'. I know that there's a wave called a 'closeout'. I know that a bloke they call Mouse tried to ride a closeout last summer. A closeout is a wave that breaks up into white water all along its length. They found Mouse out in the bay. He'd been sucked down in the surf. He couldn't remember what had happened.

"Probably got hit by his board," Gull said. "Happens more times than you think."

Then there's the story about the Big One, the monster wave they're all waiting for. A bloke called Simbo rode the Big One, last year. It came in a set of seven waves. Simbo caught the seventh wave and rode it right up the beach. He stepped off his board, and walked away. Never said anything to anyone. This was really cool. The local crew bought Simbo as much as he could drink. "Hey, Simbo!" they'd wave. "Over here!"

Stoney and I didn't care about the Big One. Today, the fish weren't biting.

"Might as well pack it in," I said to Stoney.

"Might as well," Stoney said.

We only ever catch mackerel or gurnard. A gurnard's an ugly fish, and I don't like mackerel, anyway. We always throw them back. There are no decent fish left, these days.

We packed up our rods and walked home over the cliff, avoiding the car park, as usual. I'd been telling Stoney that Gull had said the angry bloke's name was Bait. No-one knew where he came from.

The beach lay spread out like a cold, white blanket at the start of another winter. Behind us, the rip current ruffled the sea. I wished it would take me away before the boredom set in.

Already it would soon be Christmas. I could hardly imagine next year. Would I have a proper job for the first time in my life? Holiday jobs had been all right until now, but I didn't want to be doing them next summer. You can do any job for a summer. But imagine doing it forever, with winters in between.

Now I would have to think about what I wanted to do. But all I'd known was Hellbay, the shops, and the estates where I'd lived. Now that I'd left school, I was supposed to know what to do with my life, but I didn't. I didn't know what to do. I didn't know what to think.

"Feels like being shipwrecked without a life raft," I said to Stoney.

"What does?" Stoney looked at me.

"Leaving school," I said. Stoney had left school four months ago, too. "It'll soon be Christmas," I said.

Stoney knew that I was thinking about jobs. "The time goes really quickly," he said. "Even though there's nothing to do."

We both knew it wasn't true. We were kidding ourselves we had things to do. You can even get tired of fishing.

November already, I thought, when I got home. I went upstairs and looked in the mirror. Would I still be in Hellbay when I was forty, like Dad, with the best years of my life down the drain?

"Jem!" my mother called. "Fish and chips, on the table! Are you coming?"

We have fish and chips every Friday.

"Be right there!" I shouted. I ran down the stairs.

"It says here that Cornwall is one of the poorest counties in England." Dad read from the paper as he was eating his fish and chips. "Summer jobs keep wages low. That's the trouble with relying on emmets for a living."

"They're just people who come down here on holiday," I told him.

'Emmets' are tourists, or anyone who hasn't lived in Cornwall for at least forty

14

years. Some people come down here to
retire. Other people have second homes and
only come here in summer. In winter the
town's so dark it might as well be dead.

Loads of young people who can't get jobs
in the cities flood down here. They think it'll
be better to live by the seaside, even if
there's nothing to do. But they're wrong, it's
just as bad. It's just that the air is better.

There aren't any permanent jobs, not
since the electronics factory shut down.
So when I left school, I knew what would
happen. It was only a matter of time.

"What are you going to do when you leave
school?" my mother had said, as though I had
a choice.

"Company director?"

"Seriously."

"The pie factory, or international fame."
I balanced them in my hands. "Seeing as
there's probably no jobs going these days, it's
got to be signing on."

Last summer I think I was shell-shocked
from leaving school. I didn't understand what
had happened until the summer had almost
gone. I helped my mate Smudge to rent out
deckchairs. Evenings, I worked at *The Lobster
Pot*. We had live bands on weekends.
Then autumn swept the surfers away, and it
was back to the odd job here and there, and
sitting it out until next season.

Even the amusement arcades locked their
doors as winter closed in on Hellbay. The café
closed down at Devil's Point. A few snobby
surf shops stayed open, with their wetsuits
jerking outside like hanged men. My mate
Smudge tied down his deckchairs under
plastic sheeting and disappeared to sit out

the winter in a cheap bed & breakfast up the road.

The *Hungry Pilchard Café* put a 'Closed Until 1ˢᵗ March' sign outside its door. Even *The Lobster Pot* cut its evening menu, so I was out of a job. No fish could be caught in the storms. No tourists were there to eat them.

I knew I would just have to sit out the winter, like everyone else in Hellbay. The winter storms blew in off the sea and the town looked like somewhere in Russia. We were all counting the days till next summer. In the end I just watched telly all the time while the wind howled outside like a devil.

They don't call it Hellbay for nothing.

Two or three months had gone by and I'd hardly noticed the time going. You don't realise how low you're getting, when you get more and more bored all the time. I think I was sleeping my life away in front of the telly, when Stoney came round and woke me up.

Chapter 3
Bait

"Tide's out," Stoney said.

I looked up from the settee. I wasn't interested in anything.

"There's miles of sand," Stoney said. "Good time to sweep the bay."

"So?"

"So get your dad's metal detector." Stoney switched off the telly. "Come on, I've got mine."

I could hardly be bothered to get up. I took my time hunting round for the metal detector. At last I found it in a cupboard.

"Come on," said Stoney. "Let's go."

"I feel like I've been asleep for days," I said, on the way to the beach.

"You look as though you have," said Stoney. "When did you last change your clothes?"

"Tuesday," I said. "I think."

One day in front of the telly had blurred into another. I couldn't remember what I'd been doing. I couldn't tell one day from the next.

"Looking good," said Stoney. He scanned the miles of sand laid bare by a low winter tide. The wind cut through our clothes and blasted our hair off our faces. The sea looked grey and sparkling. The sky was bright and cold.

"We might be lucky today," I said. I felt better already, out on the beach. "It said on the telly that two local men found a *cache* of Roman coins the other day."

Stoney frowned. "What's a *cache*?"

"Treasure trove. Whenever anyone finds old coins, they can get money for them."

"Sure that's not 'cash'?" said Stoney.

We didn't find much treasure that day. Instead, we found trouble. But we didn't know what would happen as we began to pass our metal detectors over the sand. This was 'sweeping' the beach.

"We won't have to do this much longer," said Stoney. "There'll be work picking flowers next month."

"What kind of flowers?"

"Daffodils," said Stoney. "My brother did it last year. You can earn a hundred pounds a week. Just turn up at Anson's Field, and give your name to the gang boss."

"The gang boss?" I said.

"The person who organises it," Stoney said. "You need to get there early. Then he'll sign you up."

A hundred pounds a week sounded good to me.

We began to sweep along the high-water mark. This was where holidaymakers had sat during the summer. We swept the beach beside each other, so that we wouldn't miss any buried metal. Some of it might be valuable. Some of it was interesting, at least. Dad had found the casing of an explosive shell from the war. Once he'd found a wartime cigarette lighter with the name 'Kay Cox' on it. Our metal detectors would bleep if they sensed a tourist's lost watch in the sand.

Stoney found a steel can or two. Then we reached the pier. We recognised a few of the local surfing crew. We watched them ride the grey waves that rolled along the side of the pier.

"I suppose the pier makes the waves," Stoney said.

"I suppose," I said. "Come on."

We swept along the beach. The winter storms had thrown up a tangle of nylon ropes and fishing nets, oil, old shoes, plastic drums and bottles. It was amazing to see the amount of rubbish that the sea had thrown onto the beach. Someone had thrown it into the sea, in the first place. But they wouldn't come and pick it up.

Sometimes men in orange jackets would turn up to clean the beach. Sometimes another storm reached the rubbish, and the sea took it away again. More often than not, the rubbish stayed wherever the sea had left it, and the gulls came and picked it over.

I swept my metal detector evenly over the rubbish as I went. But the detector didn't bleep once.

"No *cache* today, then," I said, as we reached the cliffs and turned back.

"Let's try the dunes," said Stoney.

We crossed a couple of dunes and swept down the other side of them. It was hard work, in the soft, white sand, but it was here that picnickers lost things.

Stoney slid down the next dune. Before he could stop himself, he slammed into a surfboard propped against a rock. He knocked it flying, and rolled over twice in the sand before he could pick himself up.

"Hey, Stumblebum, mind what you're doing!" One of the surfies waved from the beach. We waved back. They were all right.

"All right?" I helped Stoney up. "It *was* pretty funny."

A big bloke with a dark face appeared over a dune. Of all people, it had to be him, Bait, the angry bloke from the car park, who'd accused us of breaking his aerial. He picked up the surfboard and propped it against the rock. He didn't think it was funny.
"Seeing what you can find, while the boys are out surfing?" he said, nastily.

I hadn't even noticed that the hollow we were standing in was covered in towels and wetsuits and other things belonging to the crew.

"No," I said. "Are you?"

He looked as if he'd like to hit me.

"We're metal detecting," Stoney said. Blood ran down his leg from a graze. "I didn't mean to knock the surfboard over."

"Turn out your pockets," the angry bloke said. "Let's see what you've detected," he sneered.

25

"Knock it off, Bait," said Gull, coming over the dune with his surfboard. He nodded to me. "All right, Jem?"

"We weren't doing anything wrong," I said.

"What's the trouble?" Gull said to Bait.

Bait flipped Stoney's metal detector with his foot. "Stuff goes missing," he said. "Then I find these goons snooping around."

"Stoney and Jem are all right." Gull winked at us. "Vanish, you two."

We vanished along the beach.

"Phew," Stoney said. "Let's get out of here."

We didn't understand why he was so angry with us. We put as much distance as we could between Bait and ourselves. We were glad that Gull had turned up when he did. He might not turn up next time.

Chapter 4
King of the 'Pot

That night, I heard Bait's name again, but I didn't find out much more about him. It was a Saturday night, and there was nothing to do, as usual, except sit on the wall by the chip shop. The surfies were there, eating chips. I pricked up my ears when I heard his name.

"That bloke, Bait, he's mental," someone said. "Anyone know anything about him?"

"Steer clear," someone else said.

"Says he's waiting for the Big One," said the bloke they called Mouse. "Going to beat Simbo's record. Catch those big sets this summer."

"Ever seen him surf?" someone else said.

"Can't say I have," said Mouse.

So Bait meant to catch the Big One. That's what he'd told them, anyway. Stoney and I found out where he jogged, and stayed away from the area.

February came, but it was still too early for holiday jobs. Buses were few and far between. Better jobs were so far away that I couldn't get to them, or they were asking for skills that I didn't have. I got the odd shift at *The Lobster Pot*. I helped a mate of mine move furniture into a lorry. He works for a removals firm called MOVE IT. He drives all over the country and sleeps in his lorry, so at least he gets around.

Soon café jobs would start to appear. Till then, Stoney and I could hang around with the surfies. They never seemed to worry about anything. We were getting to know the local crew. They'd buy us a Coke at the pub. But a hush would fall if Bait walked in. His face would darken until someone bought him a drink. He would gulp it down and go, and then people would start talking again. He lived alone in his camper van in Hellbay car park, waiting for summer and the Big One, lifting weights and jogging along the beach, and everyone stayed out of his way.

On the first of March, the *Hungry Pilchard Café* opened up.

"Hello, stranger," the owner, Marcie, said to me. "Haven't seen you since Christmas."

"Been staying in," I said.

"Season will soon be starting."

"Suppose."

"Cheer up. You'll get a job soon," Marcie said.

I didn't want to remember Christmas. Dad had got me a stereo from a car boot sale. He and Mum had sat and watched me while I unwrapped it.

"Where did you get this, the dump?" I said to Dad.

"Jem," Mum said. "Dad's doing his best."

"If this is your best, don't bother," I said. I wish I hadn't, now.

Later he tried to show me how it worked, but I wouldn't listen. I didn't want anything from him. Specially not second-hand.

"Rewind and Track Select works," Dad had said. "And the speakers aren't bad."

I knew I should have been grateful. I didn't think things could get worse.

Now Mum seemed to think she had to cheer me up. "Are you all right, Jem?" she asked, almost every morning, these days.

"Fine," I'd say. "Why wouldn't I be?"

I wasn't fine, at all. But it wasn't until the crew challenged me and Stoney to a shrimp-eating contest one night, that I realised I'd been depressed ever since leaving school.

We beat the surfies, that night. The townies would have been proud.

"You couldn't do it," Gull said.

"Couldn't do what?" I said.

"Win the contest." Gull pointed to a sign over the bar. The sign announced a shrimp-eating contest! The person managing to *Eat most shrimps with a toothpick in 60 seconds* would be King of *The Lobster Pot* that night, and could order any fish dinner!

"One hundred and seventy-three shrimps in 60 seconds is the record so far," Tom, the publican, said. "Think you can beat it?"

"Bring in the shrimps," said Gull. "Who's taking me on? Stoney? Jem?"

I knew he was looking at me.

"I could beat you with my eyes closed," I said.

Tom brought out the toothpicks and two big plates of shrimps. A surfer named Shooter timed us. It was between me and Gull. The person managing to eat most shrimps with their toothpick would be King of the *'Pot*, that night.

"Toothpicks at the ready." Shooter brought down his arm. "Go!"

Gull and I started stabbing shrimps and stuffing them into our mouths. It wasn't easy

to get them. They swam about on the plate.
I brought my mouth close to the plate, and
shovelled them in as fast as I could.

"Nice technique, keep it up!" Stoney
bellowed in my ear. "Go, Jem! Go, Jem!"

Gull was going well. Then he looked up.
As soon as he saw my mouth, completely
stuffed with shrimps, he exploded with
laughter. Shrimp-paste all over the place!

"The winner!" Shooter said, holding up my
arm.

Everyone was laughing and cheering. I had
beaten the record – 189 shrimps were missing
from the plate Tom had brought me! I could
have anything I wanted from the menu.
The cook brought me an enormous dinner.
I thought I was going to burst. Gull pinned a
shrimp to my sweater. Tom gave me a hat
saying 'Shrimp King'. Everyone bought me a

drink and had a joke to tell. I never wanted the evening to end. How long had it been since I'd felt that good about myself?

I walked home slowly, thinking.

It was being King of the *'Pot* for one night that made me realise something. The summer of the surfers' big wave – Big Summer – still stretched ahead of me. I had nothing to look forward to except the knowledge that it would probably be a long time before I felt as good about myself again.

Chapter 5
Albania

In March, Stoney came to collect me. "Daffodil picking," he said.

We hurried to Anson's Field, where a knot of people had gathered. It was seven-thirty in the morning, and the fields were covered in mist.

The gang boss took our names. A van pulled up and people got out. One of them was a boy of about our age.

"Right," the gang boss said. "Go up the rows picking the daffs, then down the other side. Make your stalks as long as possible. Pick only flowers that look like this." He held up a tight, green bud. "Lay the flowers that you've picked between the rows for someone else to collect. Don't pick any flowers that are already open – understand?"

The new arrivals nodded dumbly. No-one had anything to say.

"Coffee break at ten-thirty," the gang boss said. "You, you – and you – start at the bottom of the field. The rest of you, follow me."

Stoney had been put with someone else.

I found myself picking daffodils next to the boy from the van. It was backbreaking work. By the time I'd picked half a row, I had to stand up to straighten my back.

"Problems?" the gang boss roared.

He expected me to pick flowers without stopping. By the third row, my head was spinning. Sweat ran into my eyes. I could hardly see where to lay down the flowers that I'd picked.

The boy from the van picked beside me. The gang boss eyed him. He inspected the flowers from each row as they came up the hill in boxes. "Hey, Albania! Pick longer!" the gang boss shouted.

The boy from the van smiled and waved. He hadn't understood.

"He wants you to pick the flowers so that the stalks are longer." I showed him how long mine were. "Why does he call you 'Albania'?"

"I come from Albania – my home," the boy said.

"I'm Jem," I said, patting myself.

"Josef," said Josef. "I pick longer," he said.

Josef tried to pick faster and make his stalks longer. I saw him crawling along the rows. I could see that his back and legs hurt him. At the end of ten rows, I met him again. "Here," I said, "take some of mine."

I laid some of my flowers beside Josef's row. He didn't stop me, or take them. I think he was too tired. His face was white. He had rings under his eyes. The gang boss noticed us. "Work too much for you, Albania?" he said. "Perhaps you'd like to lie down."

"I am picking," said Josef.

"Faster," the gang boss replied.

Coffee break came at last. The boss came round with a thermos and gave everyone a cup of sweet coffee. Then we picked until one o'clock. Our hands got covered in sticky sap from the broken daffodil stalks. The stony soil hurt our knees. The sun came out and burned our backs. Our legs ached. Our arms got tired. It was better not to look up at the row of flowers ahead of you. No matter how fast you picked, there would be another row, and another.

When we stopped for lunch, Josef sat down. He pulled out a bag of sandwiches. For a while he sat and looked at them. I felt sick from bending double. I didn't feel hungry, either.

"Bet you wish you weren't here," I said. "Picking flowers is the worst job in the world."

"I pick tomatoes," Josef said. "Also I pick potatoes."

"What a life," I said.

Josef looked at me. He didn't understand.

"I am lucky," he said.

We picked from two until four o'clock, and I didn't meet Josef again. By the time the gang boss blew his whistle, I was picking flowers like a robot. I didn't think about what I was doing. I just knew I had to keep doing it.

We all lined up, and the boss paid us off. "I won't need you tomorrow," he said to Josef's group. "You're not picking fast enough."

The leader of Josef's group packed everyone into the van. Josef had said that he picked tomatoes and potatoes. I supposed they'd move on to another place where there was work.

"'Bye, Albania," I said, but he didn't hear me.

Josef waved once before he climbed into the van. His eyes looked unhappy, though his mouth smiled.

I watched them drive away. The van bumped along the ruts in the track and vanished at the gate. Then Josef was gone. For me, picking flowers was a bonus. For Josef, it was a way of life. His home was far away, in a country he couldn't go back to.

I went home and ate egg and chips for tea. I felt glad that summer was coming. At least then there would be work. Josef would be miles away, working wherever he could. Perhaps he slept in the van, closing his eyes and seeing his home, opening them, and saying goodbye to it. I could picture his thin shoulders now. And I knew that however bad I thought my life was, 'Albania' had it worse.

I picked flowers for the rest of that week, and I earned a hundred pounds, but it didn't make me feel any better. The memory of Josef's eyes ruined the feeling of having some money, so I spent it quickly, on stupid things, and then I was back where I'd started.

Summer was just around the corner.

Then two things happened which changed my life.

Chapter 6

Driftwood

They were both really big things. In a funny way, they were linked.

Saturday nights sometimes turned nasty as tourists flooded Hellbay. The clubs would spill out onto the streets. Sometimes there would be fights.

The night Bait punched Stoney, and Stoney almost died, I spent ten hours in the hospital. Bait had bumped into Stoney at a club, and had punched him in the side of the neck.

Bait had thought Stoney was someone else –
or so he said. Stoney had almost burst an
artery.

I waited in Casualty with Stoney's mother.
They didn't tell us much. In the end it was all
right and Stoney was out of danger.

But now it was Bait's turn to cry.

It was the morning after I'd spent the
night at the hospital, and I was walking along
the beach. A lonely surfer waited for a wave.
The morning light looked grey, though
summer had come – a summer that Stoney
would see now. No thanks to Bait, who would
be charged with attacking him, I supposed.

I was thinking so hard about the night's
events, that I almost fell over the surfboard –
a beautiful surfboard, silver and grey, floating
on little waves that seemed to tug at my feet.
It bobbed like a piece of driftwood, and no-one
seemed to have their eye on it. It didn't take

a genius to see that it was in danger of being washed away. Who could it belong to?
There was no-one else around. I gave the lonely surfer a wave.

At last he rode in and strode up the beach.

"I saved your other surfboard," I said.
"It was about to get washed away."

The surfer shook his head. "Not my board," he said. "Wish it was."

DADE COUNTY was written in red on the upper side of the surfboard. The rest of it was decorated in swirling patterns of silver, grey and white. It had gleamed like the surf itself, when it had been in the sea.

The surfer flipped it over. "Single fin. Nine feet long, at least. Heavy, too." He turned it back again. "Big rails, or outside edges. They haven't made these since the 1960s."

"What should I do with it?" I asked.

"Wait till the Beach Office opens. Take it to lost property," he said.

"And?"

The surfer shrugged. "Wait sixty days. If no-one claims it, it's yours."

Chapter 7
Sixty Days

If you've ever waited for sixty days, you'll know that it feels like a hundred. I'd found the surfboard in May. July seemed a long time in coming.

"I thought you weren't into surfing," Stoney said.

"I'm not, but – you should see it."

I told Stoney all about the surfboard.

"So where is it, then?" he said.

"Stuck in the sand," I told Stoney. "I took the board to the lifeguard. He sticks it in the sand in front of the lifeguard's hut every day, to see if anyone claims it."

"How long for?"

"Sixty days."

"Sixty days is a long time," said Stoney, trying to wiggle his feet as I sat on his bed. Sixty days was almost two months. I'd got out the calendar millions of times.

"If you count sixty days from the fourth of May, when I found it," I said, "it means that I can claim Dade County's surfboard on the first of July."

"Whose surfboard?" Stoney asked.

"Dade County's. The name's on the surfboard," I said.

"Sounds like one of those legendary surfies," Stoney said. "Dade County. I bet he's cool and rich."

48

He might come and claim his lost surfboard, I supposed. Or he might be so cool, that he'd write it off – so rich, that he'd buy another. Two months was a long time to wait to find out. Long enough for Stoney to get out of hospital. Long enough for loads of things to change.

"What should I do?" I asked Stoney.

"Wait," he said, "like me. What else can you do?"

Stoney looked under the grapes that my mother had given me for him, and found the two Snickers bars that I'd sneaked underneath them. He gave one to me and bit off the top of his.

"At least, I suppose it's mine," I said. "I mean, if no-one claims it."

"Did the lifeguard write your name in his book?" Stoney said.

"Yes."

"The board's yours," Stoney said.

It had never crossed my mind before.
A surfboard was something that other people
owned. People with long hair went surfing.
I'd never even thought of trying.

All the way home I imagined owning Dade
County's surfboard. Placing my feet in Dade
County's footsteps – if I could ever stand up
on it!

I'd never taken any interest in surfing.
I couldn't afford the gear. I wasn't in the
surfie group at school. Now I tried to
imagine what being a 'grommet' might be
like. A grommet is a beginner. I knew that
much from Gull. Old surfies on longboards
liked to ride over grommets. Then there was
the crew to think about. The crew might not
accept me. They knew I was a townie.
My mates might think I'd changed. I *would*
have to change – was I ready?

As I turned into our street, already my brain was buzzing. Could I live up to Dade County's surfboard? Did I even want to?

Dade County was one of those names. It grew on you, once you'd heard it. I started to dream he'd come knocking on my door. I dreamed he'd demand his surfboard. Other times I dreamed he'd pull up in a flash car. "Hey, dude, time to come surfing," he'd say. Then I woke up one morning and felt sure he'd left his surfboard specially for me to find.

In the end I bought a surfing magazine. Or Stoney bought one for me.

"Here," he said, handing me a magazine called *Tube!* over his bed in the hospital. "I asked my mother. She brought it in. It tells you how to surf."

I took *Tube!* home and read it. 'Tubing' meant shooting a barrel – going down the

middle of a wave. I thought I'd probably try
to stay on the top of a wave.

By now I was itching to try it.

Next morning I went to the beach.
The waves rolled over my toes and tugged out
the sand underneath them. A few of the local
crew waited in the line-up. There wasn't
much of a swell, but still I stayed to watch
them. One of them waved to me to join them.
It was frustrating. Somewhere locked in the
lifeguard's hut, Dade County's surfboard
waited for me.

I'd never taken much interest in surfing
before. But something inside me waited.
May came and went. I got a paper round and
a job in a beach café. Every day, the silver
and white surfboard stood in the sand outside
the lifeguard's hut, waiting for Dade County
to claim it. Every day I served Coke and
burgers in the beach café, waiting for some

tanned guy to take the wonderful surfboard out of my life forever. But still it didn't happen. Plenty of people admired it. But no-one claimed the surfboard.

Most of June slipped by, and Stoney was supposed to be resting at home. We watched a lot of sport on TV, and I swam a lot off the Point.

"You'd think 30 days would be enough," I complained to Stoney.

"Enough for what?" Stoney said.

"For someone to claim a surfboard."

At last the day came.

The first of July was the sixty day anniversary of the day I'd fallen over the surfboard. I went to the lifeguard's office with the piece of paper he'd given me to say that I'd found it.

"I'm Jem Butler," I said. "I've come for the surfboard."

"Sorry, mate, what surfboard?" It wasn't the usual lifeguard.

"The one that's in front of the office."

"Gone to Devil's Point," he said.

"What, you mean the dump?" My heart began to hammer. I'd been so sure of myself, I hadn't even checked to see if the surfboard was still in the sand. "But it's sixty days, today," I said. "I was told I could come and claim it."

"We cleared out the lost property yesterday. Last day of the month," he said.

I'd counted sixty days from the day *after* I'd found it. They'd cleared out lost property the day before I came for it – sixty days from the actual day I handed it in. I felt my mouth go dry. "Where is it now, then, d'you think?"

"On the lorry." The man laid down his pen. "Look, mate, it might not have gone, yet. Want to run down to The Strand?"

In moments I was running down the long road that followed the curve of the bay. At last I could see the lorry. It was loaded with bags of rubbish waiting to be taken over the hill to the dump at Devil's Point. Was that the tip of a surfboard that I could see poking out between them?

I ran as hard as I could, but the lorry didn't seem to get closer. "Hey!" I shouted. "Wait!"

Just as I reached it, the lorry shuddered to life. "Stop!" I shouted. "Excuse me!"

A man eating an apple leaned out of the cab.

"You've got my surfboard!" I waved my receipt breathlessly. "Sixty days, and I'm claiming it!"

Dade County's wonderful surfboard gleamed in the back of the lorry, between lost bicycles and bottle banks. A man in an orange jacket climbed up and handed it down. "This what you want?" he said.

"Don't you want to see my receipt?" I said. "It says here that I found it. My name's Jem Butler –"

"Your lucky day, Jem Butler."

"– and the man at the Beach Office said I could claim it, if nobody came."

The driver bit into his apple. "Take it, mate," he said.

Chapter 8
Hooked

At the last minute, I'd almost lost it. Now the surfboard was mine. All I had to do now was to live up to it. I stored the surfboard behind the shed at the side of the house, so that I wouldn't have to explain it to my parents. I couldn't explain it to myself. The board was mine, at last. Would Dade have left it behind the shed? No, he'd have started to learn to ride it as soon as possible.

Two days later I carried it down to the beach. The first thing I'd get would be a case with straps, so that I could carry the surfboard more easily.

The beach looked empty when I got there at four o'clock. One of the first rules of surfing, my mag had said, was Never Surf Alone. But I wanted to go when it was quiet. I didn't want to be laughed off the beach straight away – me, a grommet, with a drop-dead gorgeous surfboard. I'd look like an idiot when I fell off it.

Gull and a few older guys were there, when I put down the board in the sea. Gull would be on my side. I paddled out. It was hard work, using one arm, then the other, trying to look ahead to make sure that I didn't get in the way of someone riding a wave.

It wasn't too hard to get through the first few lines of white water. I arched my back, and the water ran down between me and the surfboard. Then I paddled on. The big waves

ahead looked scary, but Dade County wouldn't
have turned back, so neither would I. One or
two surfers shot past me. The water was
really cold. I hadn't got a wetsuit like they
had. A wetsuit would be the second thing I
got.

The surfboard was wide and strong.
It seemed to know what to do. Dade County's
surfboard bobbed like a swan over the waves.
It stopped where the waves broke, waiting for
me to turn it. At last a wave came along that
didn't seem too big.

I turned the surfboard and waited. Then I
saw Gull. He was waiting beside me.

My heart hammered as the wave rose.
Too late to turn back, now. The wave came
curling down on us, glassy and green, lifting
us as it came. Dade County's surfboard leapt
under it. In moments we were off, racing
down the wave. The crest of it broke behind
me, and carried me off like a bird.

59

Amazingly, I stood up first time. I couldn't believe it, myself. In one smooth movement, my feet had found a place on the surfboard. I had even walked along it, to balance at the nose! My legs and feet had done it for me – or was it the board? I'd even made a bottom turn and surfed across the wave!

"Nice going!" Gull grinned through the surf.

"Thanks!" I shouted, falling off. The wave mixed me up with the surfboard, and then I knew I had lost it. For a moment, everything was white. Being in the middle of a wave was like being in a washing machine!

When I surfaced, Gull was waiting.

"You need a leash!" He showed me the line attaching his board to his wrist. My board had gone all the way to the beach on the wave. It took me a long time to get it back. Gull waited for me. We lay on our boards and paddled out again. A leash would be the third thing I got.

"Some board," he said.

"Isn't it?" I said, proudly.

"Didn't know you surfed."

"Nor did I."

We sat in the line-up together. At last a big wave curled down.

"Make for the pocket!" Gull shouted.
The green wave towered over us.

"The pocket?" I screamed. "What do you mean?"

"The steepest bit – under the lip!"

The wave lifted us up. It seemed like the biggest wave I'd ever seen. We had to ride it or let it smash into us.

Already Gull was riding it. I paddled up the wave until I thought I'd flip over. Then I turned and dropped down the face of the wave like a stone. The nose of the silver and white surfboard cut the green water like a knife. I had never felt anything like it. I thought I was flying.

When I 'wiped out' in white water, I didn't care. When I surfaced and spotted Gull looking out for me, I could have told him not to bother.

I had found my escape from Hellbay. I felt totally comfortable on that board, confident I could ride it. The feeling of surfing down that wave was like nothing I'd ever felt before. I waved to Gull, making the diver's sign with my thumb and forefinger, meaning 'I'm OK'.

I was more than OK. I was perfect. Gull didn't need to look out for me, anymore.

I could have told him, I was in heaven.

Chapter 9
Big Summer

After that, I never looked back.
Dade County's board gave me wings.

I started to imagine what he looked like.
Big and tanned, with far-seeing eyes, careless
with expensive gear, like his surfboard.
But Dade County could afford to be careless.
Wasn't he a legend, like Laird Hamilton, a
surfer I'd seen a programme about? He must
have plenty of surfboards. He could afford to
lose one to me.

July rolled over the town like a wave, and the beaches filled with tourists. The bed & breakfasts hung 'No Vacancies' signs on their walls. Cafés and restaurants hummed. *The Lobster Pot* offered me a job five nights a week, but it got in the way of my surfing practice, so I told them 'no' and went down to the beach, most evenings.

I went down most mornings, as well. Crowds flocked down to the beach, but the summer swell was good and I got a buzz from standing up and surfing in, which I could do quite easily, now. It hadn't seemed hard to get better. It was as if a feeling for surfing had been just under my skin, waiting for me to find it. After my first ride on the silver and white surfboard, I was hooked. The rest had seemed to come naturally.

Stoney got well and sat watching me. I rented him a sunbed from my mate Smudge. In fact, Smudge gave it to me for free.

"Jem?" he said. "Jem Butler?"

"Yes?"

"I hardly recognised you, mate. Where did you get those muscles?" Smudge punched me in fun.

"Same place I got the surfboard," I joked.

Smudge nodded towards Stoney. "Stoney's changed a lot, too."

"Bait knocked him down in a club," I said. "I thought everyone knew."

"Been sleeping all winter," Smudge said. "I don't know what's going on."

"Bait's case comes up next month," I said.

"Good swell today, isn't it?" Smudge eyed the name on my surfboard. "Dade County – is that your professional name, now?"

"Dade County – yes," I lied.

"Sounds like a legend."

"I will be."

"The way you handle that board," Smudge said, "you're a bit of a legend already."

The local crew were in awe of my surfboard. No-one could ride it but me. Being called a bit of a legend by Smudge should have made me feel good. I paddled out to the line-up. What had made me say that my name was Dade County? His board felt like a part of my body. *Was* I Dade County, now?

The summer days got longer, and surfing filled my life. I was becoming part of the surfing scene. I felt like a king when I rode up the beach. I woke up thinking about surfing. I went to bed and dreamed I was surfing. Surfing was the best thing that had ever happened to me. To walk out onto that beach, with Dade County's surfboard under my arm, made me feel like ... Dade County.

The other surfers gave way to me. I usually surfed with Gull.

Then one day I read in the paper that Bait's case had come up.

"Bait got six months," I said to Gull as we sat on our surfboards, waiting for a set to roll in at the end of August. "Not much for punching Stoney's lights out."

"I had him pegged for a dangerous bloke," Gull said.

"He wasn't a surfer."

"No, he stole our stuff."

The memory of Bait hanging around in the dunes, where the surfies had left their belongings, came back to me. It had been the day Stoney had knocked over a surfboard.

Bait had been threatening, then. "What d'you mean?" I said.

"He was stealing expensive wetsuits," Gull said. "They found them in the back of his van."

"So that's why he scared us off."
I remembered the day Bait had burst out of his van and accused us of snapping his aerial. "And *he* accused *us* of thieving."

"He's a villain," Gull said. "He deserves all he gets."

"Dade County wouldn't have been scared of him," I said, without thinking.

"Sounds familiar – is he a surfer?" Gull said.

"You haven't heard of him?" I moved my leg to cover his name on my surfboard.

"Feels like I've heard the name," Gull said. "Dade County ... no, I can't place him."

Dade County wouldn't have covered up his name. Dade County would have been proud to own it. But there was no time to think about that. We caught a wave together. I made some fancy turns, and easily beat Gull to the beach. My surfboard was better and faster than any other board in the bay. I rode all the way up the beach. Stepped off the board and walked off. I could feel the crew watching me go. I felt about ten feet tall.

But the thought of Bait ruined the day. He's a villain, Gull had said. Deserves all he gets. But no-one deserves all they get, I thought later, not even my old man.

I helped Dad to turn out the garage to find some things to sell. He was desperate to hold a car boot sale to raise money. Next weekend, he'd visit other car boot sales and buy other people's rubbish. At least it would be different rubbish. That was what my dad did. Finding what he thought was a bargain was his way of feeling good about himself. Mine was surfing and practising surfing. But I didn't want to talk about that.

"You're quiet, today," my dad said.

"Yes."

"You're always quiet, these days."

"That's the way I am, now," I said.

"I liked you the way you were," he said. "At least we used to talk."

Dade was the strong and silent type, what did my dad expect? Dade didn't need anyone else. He just needed to be good at something.

That night in my room I stencilled DADE COUNTY onto a T-shirt and tried it on, for a laugh. I tried to imagine entering a surfing competition under that name, somewhere far from home, where no-one would know who I was.

I looked at myself in the mirror.

Dade would get home after a hard day's surfing and throw back a beer. He would call his buddies: *Dade here. Yeah. Meet me tonight. Did you catch those barrels, today?*

A 'barrel' was the middle of a wave. Also known as a tube. I hadn't managed to 'shoot a tube', myself. I would never be a champion surfer. But still I was better than most. By the time September came, and Smudge had begun to rope down his deckchairs under plastic sheeting, I could make some complicated turns. I was brown. I even had muscles. Dade would be proud of me. I wasn't sure who I was, or if I was proud of myself.

Big summer was fading fast. Stoney started work at the chip shop. Soon the winter winds would blow the chip papers onto the beach. The tanned surfers would disappear until next year, and the long, grey Hellbay winter would stretch ahead of us until next spring, when the daffodils came out.

I remembered Josef's grey-looking skin and the dark circles under his eyes. Would he be back again, next year? Would he recognise me, if he was?

Chapter 10
The Rip

The day I broke all the rules, I had felt so sure of myself.

Never Surf Alone was just one of the rules that I broke. I was surfing out of my depth. I wasn't a strong enough swimmer. The sea was too rough. The red flag was flying. My board was too heavy for really big waves. I wasn't wearing a wetsuit, which might have helped me to float. I wasn't wearing a leash to attach me to my board, which could have been my life raft. I hadn't done a warm-up or checked for rip currents. There were no lifeguards at the end of the season. The list went on and on.

I suppose I thought nothing could hurt Dade County. And I paddled out alone, through white water that should have warned me the surfing that day would be way beyond my ability.

Big waves crashed over me.

Still I paddled on, further than I had ever paddled before. A strong currrent was running across the bay, but I thought I could avoid it. Then the board began to bob. It began to move sideways, and there was nothing that I could do to stop it. I tried to turn, to catch a wave, but I was too far away from the beach. I could feel the surfboard being pulled out to sea underneath me. If I fell off it now, I would be pulled out, too!

I tried to see where the ruffled water ended, but it stretched as far as I could see. It made a rippling sound as it tugged me out to sea. The rip current had me in its grip! How could I have let this happen?

Keep calm, something told me. Go *with* the rip, don't fight it. Paddle over it and find a wave, my brain seemed to tell me. You've seen surfers paddle over the rip current before. Keep going. That's it. You can do it.

Going with the rip would take me further out to sea than I'd ever been before. I suddenly realised that I was gambling with my life. Would I be able to turn and paddle back?

I looked back. A tiny figure stood on the beach. Whoever it was probably hadn't seen me. The lifeguards had packed up and gone. Their hut was shut up till next season. Who would see me, if I waved for help?

Who would even know where I'd gone?
The water was dark blue, and deep, and cold.
It made a rushing sound as it pulled me so far
out to sea, that I thought I would never get
back. For a moment I felt completely alone,
the way Stoney must have felt when Bait hit
him.

Then the board seemed to turn of its own
accord.

It picked up speed as I paddled, which
made me paddle faster. I shot out of the
ruffled water made by the rip current, and a
wave rolled up underneath me and carried me
towards the beach. In moments another wave
had taken me with it, for the longest ride to
the beach that I was ever going to get. I stood
up in one, smooth movement. Between my
toes the name DADE COUNTY made me more
determined to reach the beach. For me this
was the Big One. Could I make it, now?

The wave tore on to the beachbreak and broke into white water and threw down my board, end over end. In seconds I was in the 'washing machine' in the middle of a wave again, and this time I would never touch the bottom. I didn't even know which way up I was. There was no up or down, in the white foam which filled my nose and mouth. I was being churned round and round, held down by the pressure of water, and I couldn't seem to come up, no matter how hard I tried.

How long could I hold my breath? I was sinking – going – gone!

Chapter 11
Dade County

A brown hand reached down and pulled me up through the foam. I grabbed a board – not my board. A dark head stood out against the white surf.

"Gull!" I spluttered. "You saved me!"

But it wasn't Gull. It was a girl in a wetsuit.

"Hold on," the girl said. "We can make it."

I flopped over her surfboard and held on. Together we paddled back to the beach, where no-one else had seen what had happened. The distant figure on the beach had been her. She had seen that I was in trouble, and had come out to save me.

The silver and white surfboard had been carried in by the waves.

"You went too far," she said.

"Too far out – yes." I tried to thank her, but nothing came out. I staggered up the beach and threw myself down. I knew how close I had come.

When I opened my eyes again, she was lying beside me. "Got it," she said.

"Got what?" I said, shading my eyes.

"My board back, thank goodness. Thanks a lot. I thought it had gone forever."

"What do you mean?" I said.

She was sitting on Dade County's surfboard, eating crisps. I noticed she spoke with an American accent. "You found my surfboard," she said. "You've been using it. That's OK."

"You're American."

"I was actually born here," she said. "Then my parents emigrated to America."

"To Dade County?" I said, after a moment.

"Miami-Dade in Florida, that's right," she said. "How did you know?"

I suppose she'd forgotten she'd written her address on her surfboard. But when I showed her how the sea had washed it away, all but the words DADE COUNTY, she laughed and said, "That wouldn't have gotten my board back to me, would it?"

"They wouldn't have returned it, you mean, without a full address?"

"How could they?" she laughed.
"Would you?"

"I thought Dade County was your name,"
I said, before I could stop myself.

"Dade, here. That'd be right. Like Dade's
a person." Her eyes filled with laughter.
Soon I was laughing myself. She opened her
wallet and showed me what the rest of her
address had looked like, before the sea had
washed it off her surfboard:

Kim Harvey

3830 Hales Boulevard

Miami-Dade 355710

DADE COUNTY

FLORIDA

USA

"What made me think Dade County was a person?" It seemed so ridiculous, now.

"Let's see," Kim frowned. "He's tall, and tanned, with blue eyes. Works out a lot –"

"Crushes cans with one hand."

"Drives a beach buggy," she added. "Owns a Jet Ski –"

"No," I said, "Dade's too classy for Jet Skis."

"You're right," she laughed. "I'm sorry. I guess I don't know him as well as you do."

I'd known him well, over the course of a summer. Better than I'd known myself.

"I think I've been pretty mean to my parents," I said. "I've been in a mood all summer. I think I've ignored them for weeks."

"You can make it up to them, now," Kim said. "It's never too late to change."

She had eyes the colour of a 'green', or unbroken, wave. She wasn't a bit like Dade County. The legendary surfer I'd imagined for so long had turned out to be a place – a county in the state of Florida! He wasn't even a tanned guy on a surfboard. He was a girl in a wetsuit. Nothing about Kim had anything to do with the 'Dade County' I thought I'd become.

"He's probably a millionaire," she said.

"Dade?" I said. "He's mega-rich. Fleet of motorbikes. His pool's the shape of a surfboard. Plus his house is silver and white."

She laughed, and I didn't mind her laughing at me.

"Kim's a nice name," I said.

It was good to sit there with Kim. She didn't know anything about me.

She didn't make any judgements. She sat there and ran her brown hands over the faded place on her surfboard where the rest of her address had been. I'd never noticed the faded place before. It had seemed to swirl in with the pattern.

All that had stayed had been DADE COUNTY.

I had tried to live up to it.

"So how did you lose it?" I said.

"I lost my surfboard, I lost my bag. It was one of those days," she said. She waggled her head. She was funny.

"Get many of those days?" I said.

"I do, when I stay with my aunt."

"Where does your aunt live?"

"Trelaw," she said, naming a cove on the other side of the Point.

"How often do you stay with your aunt?"

"Every summer," she said. "You can't surf in Miami."

"Why not?"

"You can, but you don't get the waves."

"So you fly here ..."

"And bring my board."

"It doesn't help," I said, "if you lose it at the beginning of the summer."

"I told you I'm always losing things." Her teeth were white when she laughed.

"It's been stuck in the sand for sixty days," I said. "How come you didn't see it?"

She showed me her teeth again. "I guess I've been away."

She knew she was lucky to get it back.

The surfboard gleamed like a shark in the sand. The board that Kim had replaced it with looked cheap and nasty beside it. I couldn't imagine losing that silver and white surfboard and not searching for it every day.

"It must have cost a packet," I said.

"I found it," she said. "Like you."

"How do you know I found it?"

"It was floating at the edge of the sea, wasn't it?" she said. "You almost fell over it. There was no-one else around."

"And you," I said. "How did *you* find it?"

Her eyes twinkled like the sea.

"I was hooked after my first ride," she said. "I was wandering along the beach when I found this surfboard. No-one seemed to know who it belonged to, so I took it out in the surf, and I managed to stand up first time ..."

"Me, too!"

"It's because of the surfboard," she said.

The sunlight flashed on the words DADE COUNTY and showed up the dents in the surfboard, where it had been hit by other boards.

"It's been around for a while," I said. "Look at those 'dings' in its side."

"Now you mention it," Kim said, "the pattern on it looks like something out of the 1960s."

"Now you mention it," I agreed.

The sun caught the swirls of silver and lit them up like fire. The board looked like something magical, lying there in the sand, waiting for someone to find it, to surf into their own big summer.

We looked at each other.

"Come on," Kim said. "Let's leave it."

And we got up together and left it there, without looking back – Dade County's silver and white surfboard, gleaming in the sand.

"What's your name?" she said, as we took the cliff path.

"Jem," I said.

She looked at me. "Weird name," she said.

"All right, it's Jeremy – blame my dad."

"Jeremy's nice," she said.

Nice of her, to lie like that. Nice, the way her hair flopped into her eyes so that she had to toss it back. Nice, the way she looked out at me from under it, before it flopped back again.

We looked back from the top of the cliff.

Pretty soon the tide came in and lifted Dade County's silver surfboard. And there it floated, on the edge of the sea, waiting for someone to find it.

Chapter 12
Kim

We e-mailed each other about surfing legends like Tim Curren, Wendy Botha and Lisa Anderson.

That summer changed my life. Me and Kim, we got on well. I wrote to her all winter. E-mailed her from the internet café. She rang, and we spoke on the phone. It didn't seem to matter how much it cost her. At Christmas I found a job in a record store. Trade was slow, but they kept me on.

I worked long hours and saved really hard. Next summer I flew to Florida. Yes, I visited Dade County!

Kim was there to meet me at the airport. She hadn't changed a bit. We swam at Daytona Beach. Had barbecues. Made ice-cream. Stayed at Kim's parents' beach house. We had a trip to the Everglades and saw the alligators, and we had a trip to Disney World. I had the time of my life. Hellbay seemed like a dream. But I knew I had to fly back there.

When I did, it seemed like a different place.

Either I had changed, or Hellbay had. It wasn't the same 'me' who landed. I had had my escape. Now that I had done it once, I knew that I could escape again. I was even glad to see Hellbay. Our beaches compared pretty well with anything Dade County had to offer.

I even got my job back. The record store isn't so bad.

Now I'm assistant manager, I'm just about running the place. Stoney DJs on weekends. Sometimes I help him out. We sampled some tracks together and made a demo tape. Stoney rapped over the top. We called it the 'Surfers' Mix'. We sent the tape to a record company. We call ourselves 'Hell 4 Leather'. As my dad says, who knows what might happen?

We even got a chance to be film extras!

A film crew arrived and set Devil's Point alight. The cliffs literally blazed for one scene. Everyone turned out to see. Then they told us that it wasn't a real fire, at all. They'd used lights to fake a fire! The film was all about smugglers. The cliffs around Hellbay had made a natural setting for a smuggling story. I'd never seen my home town as glamorous, before. Hellbay was waking up. Who knows what might happen in future?

But when I thought about what had happened to Stoney, about poor Josef's thin shoulders and grey skin, I knew I'd had a lucky break, the day I fell over Dade County's surfboard. I even thought about Bait, wherever he was. What kind of start in life had made him an angry person?

Hellbay had been good to me, after all. It had given me a place to find myself – a home, and a beach around a bay, where one day I could trip over a surfboard. It had been the kind of lucky break that only comes once in a lifetime.

I never saw Dade County's surfboard again. I hoped someone else had found it. Everyone deserves a Big Summer, at least once in their lives.

Barrington Stoke would like to thank all its readers for commenting on the manuscript before publication and in particular:

Lola Akin
Janet Armstrong
Allan Clark
Ciara Loughran
Naila Parveen
Salma Sarwar
Rachel Schon
Alison Shorrock
Anne Stockdale
Ben Yoxall

Become a Consultant!

Would you like to give us feedback on our titles before they are published? Contact us at the e-mail address below – we'd love to hear from you!

E-mail: info@barringtonstoke.co.uk
Website: www.barringtonstoke.co.uk

More Teen Titles!

Joe's Story by Rachel Anderson 1-902260-70-8
Playing Against the Odds by Bernard Ashley 1-902260-69-4
Harpies by David Belbin 1-842990-31-4
TWOCKING by Eric Brown 1-842990-42-X
To Be A Millionaire by Yvonne Coppard 1-902260-58-9
All We Know of Heaven by Peter Crowther 1-842990-32-2
Ring of Truth by Alan Durant 1-842990-33-0
Falling Awake by Vivian French 1-902260-54-6
The Wedding Present by Adèle Geras 1-902260-77-5
Shadow on the Stairs by Ann Halam 1-902260-57-0
Alien Deeps by Douglas Hill 1-902260-55-4
Runaway Teacher by Pete Johnson 1-902260-59-7
No Stone Unturned by Brian Keaney 1-842990-34-9
Wings by James Lovegrove 1-842990-11-X
A Kind of Magic by Catherine MacPhail 1-842990-10-1
Clone Zone by Jonathan Meres 1-842990-09-8
The Dogs by Mark Morris 1-902260-76-7
Turnaround by Alison Prince 1-842990-44-6
Dream On by Bali Rai 1-842990-45-4
All Change by Rosie Rushton 1-902260-75-9
The Blessed and The Damned by Sara Sheridan 1-842990-08-X

Barrington Stoke, 10 Belford Terrace, Edinburgh EH4 3DQ
Tel: 0131 315 4933 Fax: 0131 315 4934
E-mail: info@barringtonstoke.demon.co.uk
Website: www.barringtonstoke.co.uk